AND I THINK ABOUT YOU

To Jacob and Dylan, all grown up but still my little bears — R.K.

For my mom, a simple and brave woman — Y.L.H.

Text © 2022 Rosanne L. Kurstedt
Illustrations © 2022 Ya-Ling Huang

Published in Canada and the U.S. by Kids Can Press Ltd.

25 Dockside Drive, Toronto, ON M5A 0B5

Kids Can Press is a Corus Entertainment Inc. company

www.kidscanpress.com

The artwork in this book was created in watercolor and colored pencil on smooth heavyweight paper, with a touch of collage.
The text is set in Catalina Clemente.

Edited by Yasemin Uçar and Debbie Rogosin
Designed by Michael Reis

Printed and bound in Malaysia in 3/2022 by Times Offset Malaysia

CM 22 0 9 8 7 6 5 4 3 2 1

FSC
www.fsc.org
MIX
Paper from
responsible sources
FSC® C001507

Library and Archives Canada Cataloguing in Publication

Title: And I think about you / written by Rosanne L. Kurstedt ; illustrated by Ya-Ling Huang.
Names: Kurstedt, Rosanne L., author. | Huang, Ya-Ling, illustrator.
Identifiers: Canadiana 20210225912 | ISBN 9781525304590 (hardcover)
Classification: LCC PZ7.K966 An 2022 | DDC j813/.6 — dc23

Kids Can Press gratefully acknowledges that the land on which our office is located is the traditional territory of many nations, including the Mississaugas of the Credit, the Anishnabeg, the Chippewa, the Haudenosaunee and the Wendat peoples, and is now home to many diverse First Nations, Inuit and Métis peoples.

We thank the Government of Ontario, through Ontario Creates for supporting our publishing activity.

AND I THINK ABOUT YOU

Written by Rosanne L. Kurstedt

Illustrated by Ya-Ling Huang

KIDS CAN PRESS

Together, we eat breakfast.
I drink my coffee.
You scoop your milk-soaked cereal.

We get ready to leave.

At school, I wrap you in my arms and whisper, "Have a great day."

I arrive at my office.
Notice I missed a button.

Whoops!

And I think about you ...

I review my to-do list.

Check.

And I think about you ...

GLUB. GRRR. RIBBIT. PURR.

I read my emails.
I write some, too.

Click-i-ty,
Clack-a-ty.

And I think about you ...

"Once upon a time ..."

I have lunch
with my friend.

Chit-chat.
Splat!

And I think about you …

I water my plants.
They're growing
so big.

And I think about you ...

"I can get it myself."

I make copies
for a meeting.
Papers fly.

And I think about you ...

I share a project I've been working on.

And I wonder …

What are you sharing today?

I arrange some files. Hum our favorite song.

"Down by the bay ..."

And I think about you ...

I tidy my desk.

Shuffle. Sort. Stack.

And I think about you ...

I stop at the store to buy something for dinner.

And I think about you ... whipping and flipping, toasting and tasting.

At the end of the day, I wrap
you in my arms and whisper,
"What did you do today?"

"I ate pizza. I played zoo with my friends. And ... and ...

"I thought about you!"